Poppy's Teddy

First published in 2009
by Wayland

This paperback edition published in 2010 by Wayland

Wayland
338 Euston Road
London NW1 3BH

Wayland Australia
Level 17/207 Kent Street
Sydney, NSW 2000

Series Editor: Louise John
Cover design: Paul Cherrill
Design: D.R.ink
Consultant: Shirley Bickler

A CIP catalogue record for this book is available from the British Library.

ISBN 9780750259415 (hbk)
ISBN 9780750259453 (pbk)

Printed in China

Wayland is a division of Hachette Children's Books,
an Hachette UK Company

www.hachette.co.uk

Poppy's Teddy

Written by Louise John
Illustrated by Miriam Latimer

WAYLAND

"I want some pots for the garden," said Mum. "Do you like the pots?"

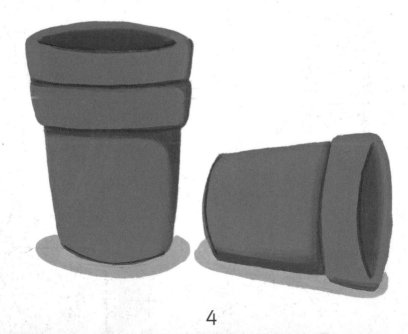

"Yes, I like them," said Dad. "I want a spade for the garden too."

"Teddy! Teddy is lost,"
said Poppy.
"I want Teddy."

"Do you like the pink flowers?" said Mum.

"No," said Dad. "I want the blue flowers."

"I have lost Teddy,"
said Poppy. "Where are
you, Teddy?"

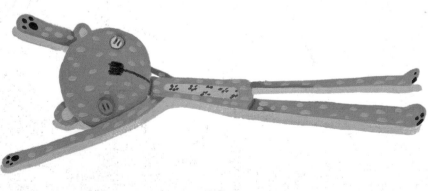

"I want some trees for the garden," said Mum. "I like the little trees."

"No," said Dad. "I want the big trees!"

"I like carrots," said Mum.
"I want some carrot seeds
for the garden."

"No," said Dad. "I want
tomato seeds for
the garden!"

"I want Teddy," said Poppy. "Teddy, where are you?"

"Oh, no," said Mum. "Teddy is lost!"

"No," said Dad. "Here is Teddy!"

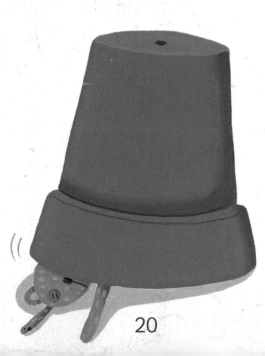

Guiding a First Read
Poppy's Teddy

It is important to talk through the book with the child before they read it alone. This prepares them for the way the story unfolds, and allows them to enjoy the pictures as you both talk naturally, using the language they will later encounter when reading. Read them the brief overview, and then follow the suggestions below:

The high frequency words in this title are:
a   are   do   for   I   is   like   no
said   some   the   want   yes   you

1. Talking through the book
Mum and Dad want to buy things for the garden, but Teddy is lost. They are too busy to listen to Poppy when she keeps telling them that she wants Teddy.

> The title of this book is Poppy's Teddy.
> Shall we look at the pictures first? Turn to page 4.
> What did Mum want to buy? Yes, some pots.
> She asked Dad, "Do you like the pots?"
> Next page: Did Dad like the pots? What did he want to buy?
> On page 8, Poppy has lost Teddy. Oh no!

Continue through the book, guiding the discussion to fit the text, as the child looks at the illustrations.

> On page 18, Mum realises that Teddy is lost.
> On page 20, Dad finds Teddy – "No, here is Teddy," said Dad. Where was Teddy hiding?

22

2. A first reading of the book

Ask the child to read the book independently and point carefully underneath each word (tracking), while thinking about the story.

Work with the child, prompting them. Praise their careful tracking, attempts to correct themselves and their knowledge of letters, sounds and punctuation, for example:

I like the way you read that like a question. Look at the flowers in the picture – this word here starts with 'p'. Now sound it out and check the picture again (p-i-n-k). What colour are the flowers? First you said 'went' but that didn't make sense, so you changed it to 'want'. Does it make sense now? Yes, well done!

3. Follow-up activities

- Select two high frequency words, and ask the child or group to find them throughout the book. Discuss the shape of the letters and the letter sounds.

- To memorise the words, ask the child to write them in the air, then write them repeatedly on a whiteboard or on paper, leaving a space between each attempt.

4. Encourage

- Reading the book again – with expression.

- Drawing a picture based on the story.

- Writing one or two sentences using the practised words.

START READING is a series of highly enjoyable books for beginner readers. **The books have been carefully graded to match the Book Bands widely used in schools.** This enables readers to be sure they choose books that match their own reading ability.

Look out for the Band colour on the book in our Start Reading logo.

The Bands are:

Pink Band 1

Red Band 2

Yellow Band 3

Blue Band 4

Green Band 5

Orange Band 6

Turquoise Band 7

Purple Band 8

Gold Band 9

START READING books can be read independently or shared with an adult. They promote the enjoyment of reading through satisfying stories supported by fun illustrations.

Louise John is really the editor of Start Reading, but wanted to see how she liked writing books, too. It was quite tricky, but she found that eating lots of chocolate biscuits made her think better! She tries out her ideas on her daughter, Amelia, who tells her if they are any good or not!

Miriam Latimer enjoys illustrating and writing stories for children. She carries her sketchbook and pens with her everywhere she goes, which make her handbag very heavy. She likes to sketch people in cafés and train stations but, if they notice, she pretends to be drawing something else!